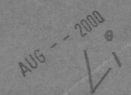

IN THE TIME
OF THE DRUMS

To Aron and Zachary, who are my heart, and to Hank, its rhythm
—K.S.

To Pop-Pop, who I'll always remember as strong-strong
—B.P.

3   5   7   9   10   8   6   4   2

This book is set in 14.5-point Opti Magna Carta.
Book design by Christy Hale

Library of Congress Cataloging-in-Publication Data
Siegelson, Kim L.
In the time of the drums/Kim L. Siegelson; illustrated by Brian Pinkney.
p. cm.
Summary: Mentu, an American-born slave boy, watches his beloved grandmother, Twi, lead
the insurrection at Teakettle Creek of Ibo people arriving from Africa on a slave ship.
ISBN 0-7868-0436-X (trade)—ISBN 0-7868-2386-0 (lib. bdg.)
1. Slavery—United States—Insurrections, etc.—Juvenile fiction.
[1. Slavery—Insurrections, etc.—Fiction.   2. Afro-Americans—Fiction.
3. Ibo (African people)—Fiction.   4. Grandmothers—Fiction.]
I. Pinkney, J. Brian, ill.   II. Title.
PZ7.S56657In   1999   [Fic]—dc21   98-30347

IN THE TIME
OF THE DRUMS

KIM L. SIEGELSON ◆ Illustrated by **BRIAN PINKNEY**

 JUMP AT THE SUN · HYPERION BOOKS FOR CHILDREN · NEW YORK

IN THE LONG AGO TIME BEFORE NOW, on an island fringed by marsh meadows and washed by ocean tides, men and women and their children lived enslaved. This was the time when giant live oaks trembled with the sound of drums and, say some, it was a time when people could walk beneath the water.

Used to be, in those early days, ships as big as barns would land at a dock on a bluff near Teakettle Creek: pirate ships with treasure to bury, cargo ships filled with cinnamon, slave ships bringing African people to do work on plantation farms.

Some of those Africans came knowing how to carve wood and make sweet-grass baskets and goatskin drums. With those things they reminded themselves of home. Wished to go back there.

One boy, name of Mentu, had never known Africa or longed for it. He was an island-born boy.

Mentu could scoot to the top of a live oak faster than a brush-tail squirrel. Could lift a black iron skillet above his head with one hand, even though he still wore shirttails. "Look how strong I am!" he would say to his grandmother, Twi.

Twi would smile and cluck her tongue at him. "Stop your foolin' lest the overseer catch you, sir. Your time for strong will come soon enough."

"When?" Mentu would ask. Twi would not say.

Mentu had always lived with Twi. The islanders, black and white, all feared her.

Africa had been her birthplace.

There, she had learned powerful root magic at her own
grandmother's knee. Ibo conjure woman, the islanders called her.
"Older than anyone living," they said. But Mentu paid them no mind, had
only known kindness from Twi. You see, Twi loved Mentu like her own soul.
Like the faraway rivers and mountains of her native land. Some said his first
breath had come from her own mouth. That as a new babe he had
been still until she whispered the secret of life onto his tongue.
He had wailed at the truth of it and waved his fists at her, and
at the charm bag she held out to him. "Not with fists,"
she had said, gathering him against her chest.
"Listen close and learn how to be strong."
He had slept to the sound of Twi's heart.

Every day Mentu went with Twi to take water to the fields. Could carry two full buckets by himself. Strong as that made him seem, he was a mischief-making boy-child all the same.

"The bucket handles pinch my hands," he sometimes complained to Twi. "You carry the water for me today."

"Nawsir!" she would say and cluck her tongue. "Twi can't be taking up your burden from you. Look out to the field workers when your hands is aching and count your luck. Soon it will be your time to be strong-strong and Twi won't be helping you then."

"How will I know when to be strong-strong if you don't tell me?" Mentu asked.

Twi still would not answer. She knew many secrets. She shared only what she wanted.

Mentu looked to the fields and watched the people bend beneath the blistering sun to slave in soil planted with cotton and cane and blue indigo seed. Saw how they worked from dark of morning to dark of night harvesting what they could not keep.

Twi told him that the long, hard work had broken them. Made memories of Africa sink so far back in their minds that they could no longer be reached. The old ways had slowly slipped away and been left behind like sweat drops in a newly plowed row.

But Twi remembered the time before.

Spoke the old words to herself in the morning while she worked. Sang African songs to Mentu in the afternoon until he could sing them back. At dinner, told him old stories so rich that he could almost smell the sweet-scented air of her homeland. Put the skin drum between her own knees and taught him ancient rhythms until they felt as natural to him as his own heart beating.

Then, come a day so hot even the gnats hushed their whining to sit among the tree shadows. In that breathless quiet, Mentu and Twi filled their buckets with well water. But before they could carry them to the fields they heard the sound of drums beating from the far end of the island. *Bop-boom-boom! Bop-boom-boom!* It was a message in rhythm that meant "A ship is come! A ship is come!"

Mentu beat his own drum. *Be-e-bow. Be-e-bow.* "We hear. We hear." He and Twi gathered with everyone else at the bluff to see what the ship had brought. It flew a Spanish flag, but it did not carry gold or jewels or sweet spices from India. The ship held a whole village of Ibo people from the African kingdom of Benin. They had been captured by the ship's owners and brought to the island to be sold.

Their ride across the ocean passage had been long, with many days spent in airless dark beneath the pitching decks of the ship.

When the ship docked at the bluff, the Ibo people could no longer hear the crash of ocean waves; only the groan of the ship, the flapping sails, and their own harsh breathing. They trembled and waited quietly, listening to learn something of their fate. Through the wooden side of the ship came the sound of the island drums. The music of Africa.

"Has some magic brought us home?" they cried. They drummed an answer using their feet on the wooden floor.

Mentu heard the rumble of their pounding feet, and it spoke to
him like the beating of his heart. "We are home! We are home!"
the people drummed. But they were far from home.

Mentu and Twi watched the Ibo people brought up from
the dark hull of the ship into the light. Saw how they squinted into
the sun. How they looked out over the unfamiliar marsh meadows
in despair. The ship had not returned them to Africa. Would never
take them home again.

Try as the ship's captain might to make them move, the Ibo people refused to set a foot on the island. Mentu turned away when the overseer lashed them with his whip. But the people would not budge for the whip. Just joined their hands tight together and began to chant a song in their own language.

Mentu listened as though his soul lived in his ears. He heard Twi's music in their song. Old words from the place where she had been born.

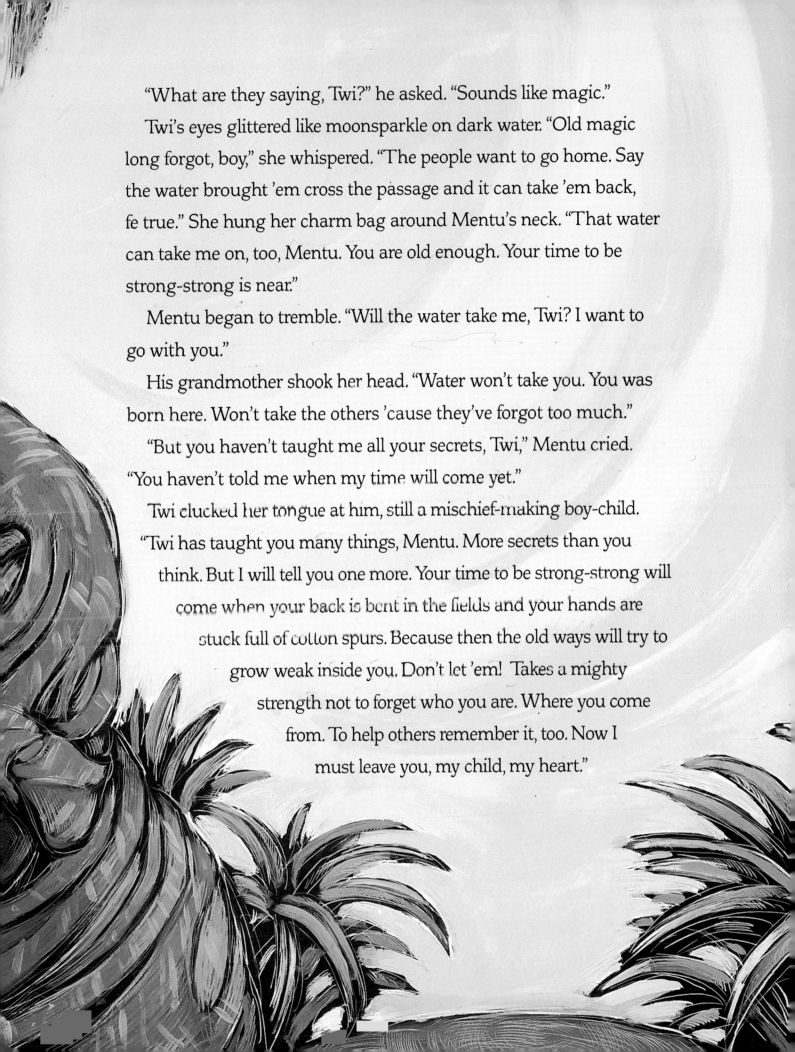

"What are they saying, Twi?" he asked. "Sounds like magic."

Twi's eyes glittered like moonsparkle on dark water. "Old magic long forgot, boy," she whispered. "The people want to go home. Say the water brought 'em cross the passage and it can take 'em back, fe true." She hung her charm bag around Mentu's neck. "That water can take me on, too, Mentu. You are old enough. Your time to be strong-strong is near."

Mentu began to tremble. "Will the water take me, Twi? I want to go with you."

His grandmother shook her head. "Water won't take you. You was born here. Won't take the others 'cause they've forgot too much."

"But you haven't taught me all your secrets, Twi," Mentu cried. "You haven't told me when my time will come yet."

Twi clucked her tongue at him, still a mischief-making boy-child. "Twi has taught you many things, Mentu. More secrets than you think. But I will tell you one more. Your time to be strong-strong will come when your back is bent in the fields and your hands are stuck full of cotton spurs. Because then the old ways will try to grow weak inside you. Don't let 'em! Takes a mighty strength not to forget who you are. Where you come from. To help others remember it, too. Now I must leave you, my child, my heart."

Then Twi kissed Mentu fast as a dragonfly. Took off running. And as she ran, the years melted from her like butter on an ash cake. Her back drew up straight. Her hair grew dark and thick with braids, and her skin smoothed until she looked like the young woman who had been taken from Africa those many years before. The islanders feared Twi more than ever when they saw this happen and they fell back to let her pass. No one tried to stop her.

From the bluff she held her hands out to the Ibo people on the dock and spoke to them. "Come with me, my brothers and sisters. I will take you home."

Mentu wept as the people crossed the dock to join the young Twi on the land. The slave catchers tried to slip ropes around their necks and arms to hold them back, but couldn't. The ropes slipped through flesh and bone like it was smoke and seawater.

Twi clasped hands with the Ibo people and led them down the bluff to the water's edge. "Twi!" Mentu called out to her, but she would not turn back, even for him.

She chanted as she led the people waist deep into the waters of Teakettle Creek. Mentu wiped away his tears and chanted with her in a voice as strong as he could make it, "The water can take us home. The water can take us home." He tried to run to her but found his feet fastened to the land so that he could not move.

Twi and the other Ibo people lifted their faces to the sky as water crept over their shoulders and then their necks. But they kept walking, as their chains snapped away. "The water can take us home," they sang. "It can take us home."

Their song disolved into bubble and foam as Teakettle Creek
swirled over the tops of their heads. Mentu's feet suddenly pulled
away from the ground and he ran to the water, but he couldn't see
Twi or the Ibo people beneath its surface.

In time, Mentu swore to everyone left behind that Twi and the
Ibos had walked all the way back to Africa on the bottom of the
ocean; pulling each other along the sandy floors, pushing aside
seaweed like long grass.

"But their chains and their song will never leave Teakettle Creek,"
others said. "And the water there will always be salty as tears."

The islanders called that place Ibo's Landing.
Stopped fishing there and never cast another net in
Teakettle Creek for fear of pulling up those chains sunk
deep in soft gray mud. Shivered when snowy egrets rose from
the marsh grass like spirits in the evening.

As for Mentu, he learned to be strong-strong in the fields beneath
the blistering sun, just as Twi had told him. He sang her old songs
to himself while he worked and to his children until they could sing
them back to him. He told stories so rich that they wondered if he had
lived in Africa himself. And he played rhythms on the skin drum
until they felt their own hearts beat in time. Gave them their own
drums and they all played together, Mentu and his children.

And they taught their own children, and they taught theirs,
through slave time and freedom time and on up until now time.

Fe true, it takes a mighty strength not to forget.

Author's Note

In the Time of the Drums is based on an oral account that has been passed down through generations of African-American communities near the Sea Islands of Georgia and South Carolina. I first heard the story from my maternal grandmother, who told it as a ghost story. Most often the tale is recalled as a fragment of memory or as a short legend. One such telling can be found in the book *Drums and Shadows,* published by the University of Georgia Press.

Many Sea Island communities claim the event. Most of these have ties to the Gullah people, or as some Gullah people refer to themselves, Saltwater Geechee people. The exact derivation of the word *Gullah* is unknown, but linguists and social historians have traced its origin to the slave trade. During that time, Gullah came to denote Africans brought from Angola. Now it refers to the descendents of enslaved black Sea Islanders and their unique culture.

Among slaves, the Gullah were often credited with supernatural powers: the ability to work magic, to control inanimate objects, to fly. As the tale is typically told, the Ibo people chose physical death, or "a slave's freedom," when they walked into the river. Indeed, for many Africans the appearance of physical death did not signal an end. Only then could the spirit find release to travel back across the Middle Passage to the shores of home. Enslaved Africans were people empowered by faith, conviction, and hope. As a storyteller, I extended their powers to include the ability to walk beneath water.

With these things in mind, I settled myself beside the waters of Dunbar Creek at the place designated as Ibo's Landing, on St. Simons Island, and listened for the chains to rattle; for the water to speak. *In the Time of the Drums* is the story I heard.

—Kim Siegelson